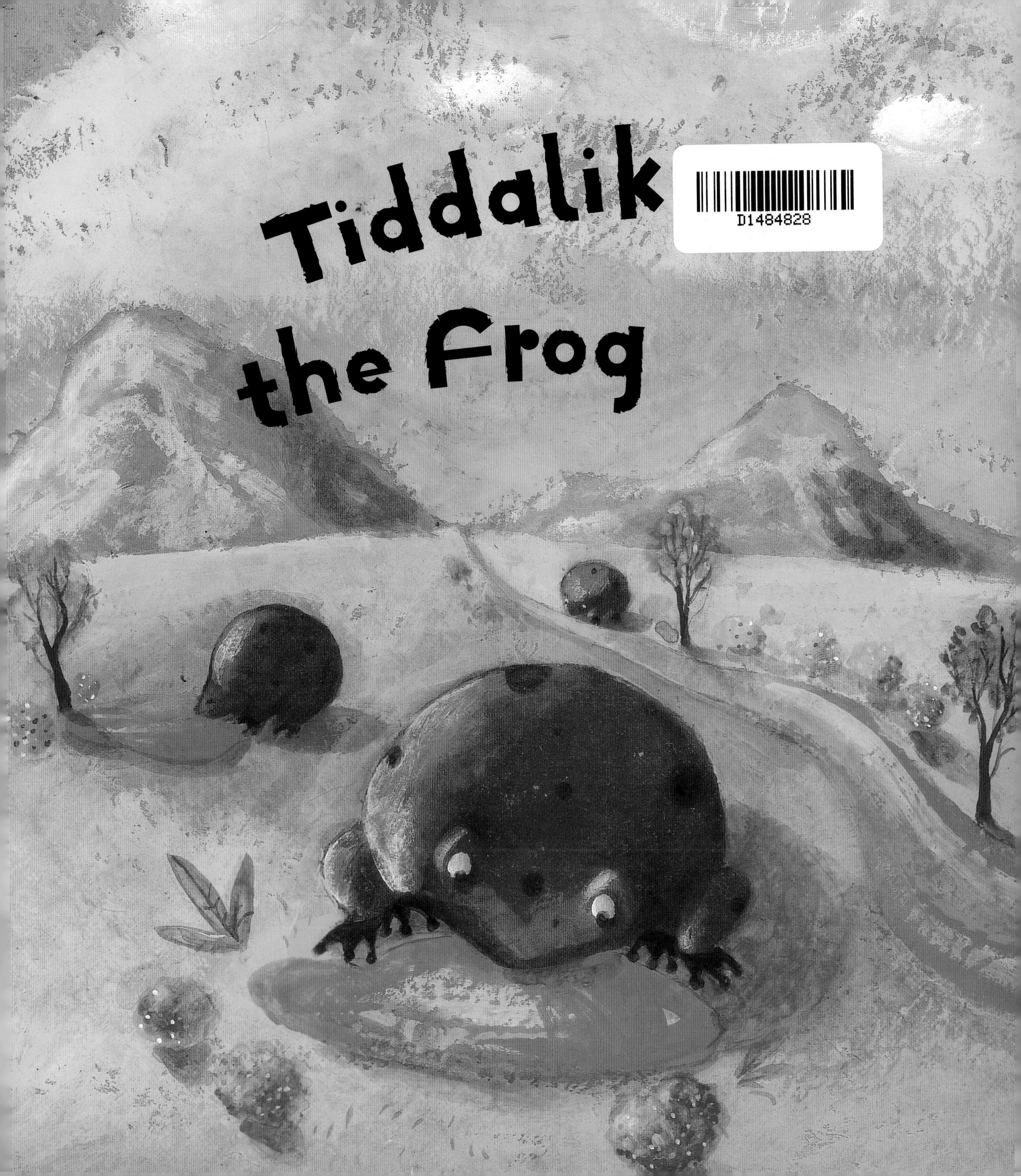
Tiddalik the Frog

Silver Dolphin Books
An imprint of the Baker & Taylor Publishing Group
10350 Barnes Canyon Road, San Diego, CA 92121
www.silverdolphinbooks.com

ISBN-13: 978-1-60710-357-8
ISBN-10: 1-60710-357-5

Manufactured, printed, and assembled in Guangdong, China.

1 2 3 4 5 15 14 13 12 11

Written by Anne Faundez
Designed by Louise Morley
Illustrated by Sanja Rescek

Tiddalik the Frog

Anne Faundez

San Diego, California

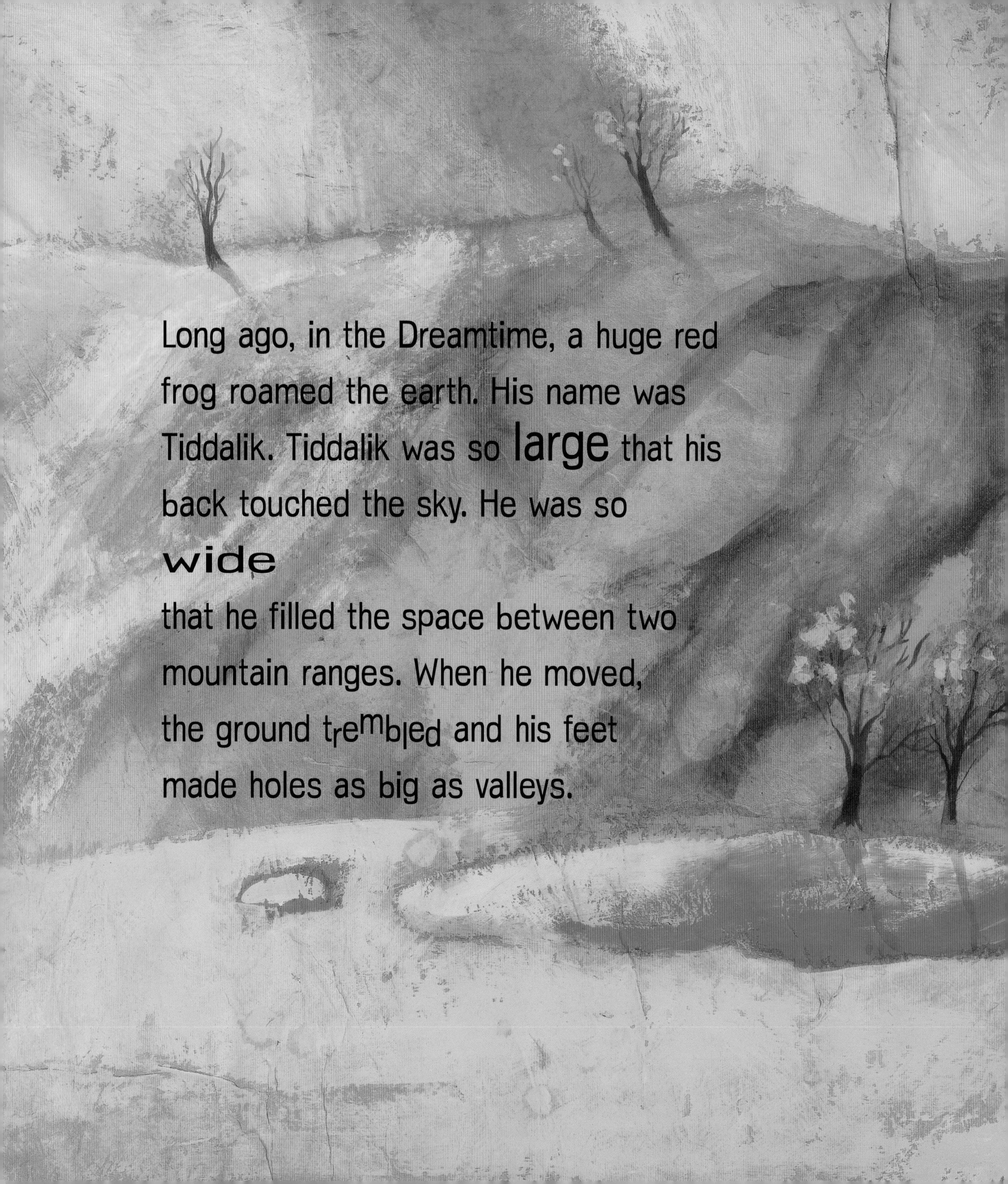

Long ago, in the Dreamtime, a huge red frog roamed the earth. His name was Tiddalik. Tiddalik was so large that his back touched the sky. He was so

wide

that he filled the space between two mountain ranges. When he moved, the ground trembled and his feet made holes as big as valleys.

One day, he woke up from a very bad sleep. He was VERY, VERY grumpy! He was also VERY, VERY thirsty!

"WATER! WATER!" he bellowed.
His words made the clouds crackle with thunder.

He found a river and drank up all the water.
He found a lake and emptied that, too.
He kept on drinking until every waterhole
was dry.

Tiddalik was now bulging with water and ready to burst.

He was too uncomfortable to move. He shut his eyes and fell into a long, deep sleep.

The days went by.

Tiddalik slept.

There was no sign
of rain in the skies.

The sun scorched
the earth. The
grasses withered
and the trees lost
their leaves.

The beautiful green
earth became hard
and cracked.

Kangaroo, Kookaburra, and Platypus were anxious. They had watched Tiddalik drinking up all the water. Now their land was turning to dust.

"The earth is so cracked that I can't hop around anymore," grumbled Kangaroo.

"There's nowhere for me to swim," moaned Platypus.

"Tiddalik MUST return our water!" said Kookaburra.

But the animals were scared to talk to Tiddalik. He was still so grumpy!

"I know," said Kookaburra. "Let's make him laugh. Then he'll spill out the water."

So Kookaburra flew right up to Tiddalik. She sang some funny songs. She wriggled and jiggled and danced about.

Tiddalik opened one eye. He shut it again.

Platypus went up to Tiddalik. She told a few jokes and then she flipped and flopped and shuffled about.

Tiddalik opened the other eye.
He shut it again.

Next, it was Kangaroo's turn.
He loved to show off. He twirled
and whirled, and thumped and bumped
his tail around.

Tiddalik opened both eyes.
He shut them again.
He was still bored.
Just then, Little Eel came rushing

towards the animals.

"Let me make Tiddalik laugh!" he cried.

He raced towards Tiddalik, turning somersaults all the way.

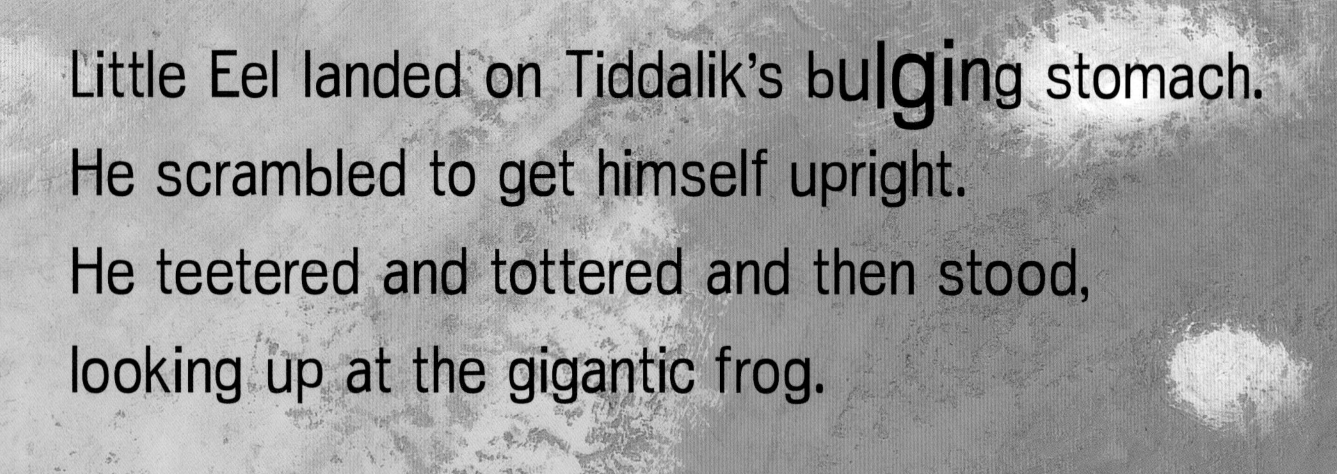

Little Eel landed on Tiddalik's bulging stomach.
He scrambled to get himself upright.
He teetered and tottered and then stood,
looking up at the gigantic frog.

Tiddalik opened his eyes. He was
so astonished to see Little Eel,
all shivering and shaking, sitting
right on his belly.

Tiddalik made a rumbling noise.
He chuckled—and a trickle of water
dribbled from his mouth.

He chuckled a bit more.

Soon, he was rumbling with laughter.
Water spilled from his mouth and ran down his sides. Tiddalik couldn't stop laughing at the sight of Little Eel sitting on his belly.
As he laughed, he felt less grumpy.

Soon, the land was awash with water.
The grasses began to grow again, and tiny leaves began to cover the bare branches of the trees.

And do you know what? To this day, Tiddalik has never again emptied the land of water.

Why?

Well, Little Eel knows just what to do now when Tiddalik gets grumpy...
and thirsty!

Can you remember?

Can you remember the names of these animals?

How did Tiddalik feel when he woke up from a very bad sleep?

How did Kookaburra try to make Tiddalik laugh?

Who finally made Tiddalik laugh?